ZOO

BY K.C. KELLEY

AMICUS READERS • AMICUS INK

Amicus Readers and Amicus Ink are imprints of Amicus
P.O. Box 1329, Mankato, MN 56002
www.amicuspublishing.us

ISBN: 978-1-68151-308-9
PB ISBN: 978-1-68152-264-7
EBook ISBN: 978-1-68151-344-7

Library of Congress Cataloging-in-Publication Data
Names: Kelley, K. C., author.
Title: Zoo / by K.C. Kelley.
Description: Mankato, MN : Amicus, [2018] | Series: Field trips, let's go!
Identifiers: LCCN 2017022318 (print) | LCCN 2017027571 (ebook) | ISBN 9781681513447 (pdf) | ISBN 9781681513089 (library binding : alk. paper) | ISBN 9781681522647 (pbk. : alk. paper)
Subjects: LCSH: Zoos--Juvenile literature. | Zoo animals--Juvenile literature.
Classification: LCC QL76 (ebook) | LCC QL76 .K45 2018 (print) | DDC 590/.73--dc23
LC record available at https://lccn.loc.gov/2017022318

Editor: Sara Frederick
Designer: Patty Kelley
Photo Researcher/Producer: Shoreline Publishing Group LLC

Photo Credits:
Cover: kali9/iStock.com
Adobe Stock: Robert Kneschke 15. Alamy Stock Photo: Peter Forsberg 3; Dreamstime.com: Stefano Panzeri 4, Verastuchelova 9, Belizar 10, Bjorn Hovdal 16T, Anna Krivitskaia 16R, David Smith 16B. Shutterstock: gorillaimages 6, Romrodphoto 12.

Printed in China.

HC 10 9 8 7 6 5 4 3 2 1
PB 10 9 8 7 6 5 4 3 2 1

A zoo teaches about animals.
Let's visit a zoo today!

This zoo has many animals. What will we see first? Amir and Penny spot an ape!

Zoo workers
show us animals.
Berta loves
the snakes!

We can touch
some animals.
Annie feeds a goat.

When animals are sick, they need help. Zoo doctors help this wolf pup.

Animals get hungry. Zookeepers feed them. Dan helps. He feeds the giraffe.

What a great day at the zoo! What was your favorite animal?

THINGS TO SEE AT A ZOO

penguin

zookeeper

lion